Chapter One

A Squeaky Sort of Chirping Sound

Jasmine Green and her best friend Tom were sitting on a wobbly wooden platform made of planks, balanced in the branches of a big old oak tree. It was a Friday afternoon in the middle of August, and it had been raining for days. It wasn't raining at the moment, but the cloudy sky hung low over the fields like a heavy grey blanket.

From their tree house, Jasmine and Tom could see the whole of Oak Tree Farm. The farmyard, with its barns and sheds, and the long, low farmhouse with its red-tiled roof. The woods

1

in the distance. The fields all around, dotted with cows and sheep. Jasmine's pet pig, Truffle, snuffling in the orchard. Her little brother, Manu, and his best friend, Ben, digging a hole in the mud by the tool shed. And, just below the tree, snaking off into the distance, the winding river that ran right through the farm.

The tree house was their new idea. So far, it consisted only of the plank platform and a rickety wooden ladder propped against the lowest branch. A rope hung down from a smaller branch. Tied to the other end of the rope, on the wet grass, was a basket containing apples, biscuits and a bottle of juice.

"OK," said Jasmine. "Pull very slowly."

Tom took hold of the rope and cautiously

For Luke
H. P.

For Gem
E. S.

First published in the UK in 2019 by Nosy Crow Ltd
The Crow's Nest, 14 Baden Place,
Crosby Row, London SE1 1YW, UK

Nosy Crow and associated logos are trademarks and/or registered
trademarks of Nosy Crow Ltd

Text copyright © Helen Peters, 2019
Cover and illustrations copyright © Ellie Snowdon, 2019

The right of Helen Peters and Ellie Snowdon to be identified
as the author and illustrator respectively of this work has been asserted
by them in accordance with the Copyright, Designs
and Patents Act 1988.

3 5 7 9 10 8 6 4 2

A CIP catalogue record for this book will be available from the British Library.

Printed and bound in Great Britain by Clays Ltd, Elcograf S.p.A.

Papers used by Nosy Crow are made from wood grown in
sustainable forests.

ISBN: 978 1 78800 156 4

www.nosycrow.com

hauled up the basket. The contents rolled to one side, the basket tipped up and the bottle and apples dropped on to the grass.

"Oh, well," said Tom. "We've still got the biscuits."

"I'll get the other stuff," said Jasmine.

The ladder wasn't too bad, as long as you didn't step on the broken rungs. Jasmine stuffed the bottle and the apples in her coat pockets, and was about to climb up again when a sound caught her attention. It was a loud, regular, squeaky sort of chirping sound, and it came from somewhere on the riverbank. "Listen," she said. "What bird is that?"

"I think it's a distress call," said Tom. "It's not normal birdsong."

"It sounds like it's coming from those brambles," said Jasmine, pointing to a patch of thick undergrowth on the riverbank. "Maybe it's stuck."

"Let's investigate," said Tom.

He climbed down the ladder and they walked to the riverbank. The rain had made it very slippery, and they had to inch down sideways, digging the edges of their wellies into the mud to stop themselves from slithering into the fast-flowing water.

They came to the edge, where the steep bank ended in a narrow ledge before plunging into the river. Tom was on one side of the bramble patch and Jasmine on the other. The desperate squawking sounded even more distressed from here.

"I'm sure it's in there somewhere," said Jasmine, looking apprehensively into the brambles. "I wish we had gloves."

Tom plunged his hands into his jacket pockets and pulled out a pair of crumpled gloves.

"Ta da!" he said. "Still there from winter."

"That's lucky," said Jasmine. "You investigate first, then I'll borrow them and look on this side."

5

As Tom crouched down and gingerly parted the brambles, Jasmine looked along the riverbank. There was a heap of stones and pebbles just above the water level below her.

Suddenly, a movement caught her eye.

It was an animal with brown fur, sitting on the stones.

"Tom," she whispered.

He looked up enquiringly and she pointed to the little creature.

"What?" said Tom. "I can't see anything."

The animal lifted its head up, looked directly into Jasmine's eyes and gave a loud squeak.

"Oh!" she gasped. "It's a baby otter!"

Chapter Two
We Don't Have Much Time

Tom's eyes widened. "An otter? Really?"

The otter squeaked again. Tom crept around the edge of the brambles and crouched beside Jasmine.

"Wow," he whispered.

For a moment they looked at it in silence, trying to take in the extraordinary fact that there was a real live otter cub in their part of the river.

"Have you ever seen one before?" whispered Tom.

Jasmine shook her head. "Never. I think they're

really rare."

"It's definitely a baby, isn't it?" said Tom. "Where are its parents?"

Jasmine leaned out across the water.

"What are you doing?" said Tom, clutching her arm. "Don't fall in!"

Jasmine continued to peer over the edge. "I'm looking for a hole that might be its home."

"Can you see one?"

"No. There's nothing. Just a solid cliff of mud."

"So what's a baby otter doing alone on that pile of stones?"

Jasmine looked at the murky water rushing beneath her. "Maybe it got swept away from its family."

"And then scrambled up on those rocks," said Tom. "And now it's calling out to its family to come and rescue it."

"But what if they don't come?"

"Let's stay and watch," said Tom. "If they don't come in a while, one of us can run back to the

house and ask your mum what we should do."

"I wonder if she's ever seen an otter," said Jasmine.

Jasmine's mum was a vet, so she had encountered many different animals close up, but Jasmine had never heard her mention treating an otter.

The otter cub was still making its distress calls.

"Its family should definitely hear it if they're nearby," said Tom. "It's so loud."

Crouched by the brambles, Jasmine studied the cub as the cold grey water swirled around the stones.

It had a broad furry head, with big round dark eyes and little rounded ears. Its black nose was like a dog's, and it had a row of white whiskers on either side of its face. Its sleek furry body ended in a thick tail. There was a patch of whiter fur, like a bib, on its throat.

They waited for a long time, watching the cub and casting their eyes anxiously up and down the

river to see if its mother was coming.

"What if the mother has abandoned it?" said Jasmine. "How long do you think we should wait? It might be really hungry."

A gust of wind blew across the water, stirring up ripples and waves. All of a sudden, a wave splashed over the stones where the otter was sitting. With a desperate squawk, the cub slithered off the stones and into the river.

"Oh, no!" cried Jasmine, springing up and staring in horror as the little otter disappeared beneath the rushing water.

"It's being carried downstream," said Tom, scrambling to his feet. "Let's go to the bridge. We might be able to get it from there."

They scrabbled up the bank and raced down the field, keeping pace with the baby otter as it struggled against the current, sometimes with its head above the water, sometimes completely submerged.

They headed for the wooden bridge near the

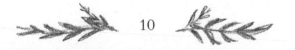

bottom of the field. Jasmine ran to the middle of the bridge and climbed over the railings.

"Hold on to my ankles," she said. "I'll try to catch it as it comes under."

"I'm not dangling you head first into the river," said Tom. "It's too dangerous."

"It'll be fine," said Jasmine. "You're strong. Just keep hold of my ankles."

Facing the river, she reached her hands behind her back and gripped the bottom rail while she lowered herself down until she was kneeling on the edge.

"Grab my ankles," she said. "I'm going to fish it out."

"It's too late," said Tom. "Look."

Jasmine gave a cry of despair as she saw the little otter, its head just above the water, disappearing under the bridge. She got up and ran to the other side. Just beyond the bridge, the river rounded a bend, where a huge weeping willow tree trailed its delicate branches into the

water. As they watched, the little otter was swept into the branches.

"Run!" said Jasmine.

They ran off the bridge and part-scrambled, part-slid their way down the bank above the

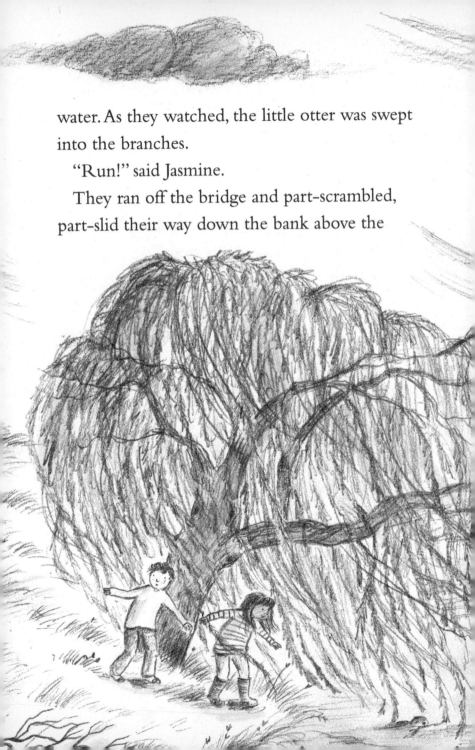

willow tree, clutching the branches to stop themselves from tumbling into the river.

The cub seemed to have given up struggling. It was floating on the surface, frighteningly still, tangled in the willow.

"It's exhausted," said Jasmine. "We don't have much time."

"We need a long stick," said Tom, "to hook it in."

"Good idea."

Tom was inspecting sticks. "Too short," he muttered, as he kicked one aside. "Too thin," he said, rejecting another.

He picked up a thicker stick and bent it. It snapped in half.

"Too brittle."

Jasmine picked up a longish curved stick. She bent it and it didn't break.

"It's a bit thin," she said, "but we don't have much time and I can't see anything better."

She unzipped her raincoat, pulled it off and dropped it on the bank. Then she took off her jumper.

"What are you doing?" asked Tom.

Jasmine pulled off her wellies and socks. "I'll try to drag it to the bank with the stick, but if I can't do that, I'll have to get in the water. If we don't rescue the cub right now, it will die."

Chapter Three
It's Not Working

A tree root, just the right thickness for a hand to grasp, arched out of the ground near the water's edge. Tom held on to the root and Jasmine held on to Tom's hand as she climbed down the muddy bank. Both of them stretched as far as they could. With her other hand, Jasmine positioned the stick on the far side of the baby otter and pulled.

But, however hard she pulled, the cub didn't move towards her. It just turned round and round in the water.

15

"It's not working," said Jasmine. "Its body's moving, but its head's stuck in the branches."

"Try again. See if you can hook its head," said Tom.

"I'll try, but I don't want to hurt it."

She manoeuvred the stick behind the otter's head. Then she turned to Tom.

"I'm scared to pull," she said. "What if I hurt its eye?"

"I don't think you will. Look, its eyes have closed."

Jasmine looked.

"That's a bad sign," she said. "We need to get it quickly."

She pulled on the stick, but the otter's head stayed stubbornly stuck. She kept trying, but she couldn't dislodge the cub from the tangle of branches.

Jasmine's parents had warned her many times never to go in the river.

"It's very fast-flowing," her dad had told her,

"and the bottom is thick silt. You could easily be carried away by the current, and if you tried to stand up, your feet would sink into the mud. It's far more dangerous than it looks."

Now, Jasmine looked up at Tom.

"I'm going to get it," she said.

Tom looked alarmed. "You can't go in on your own. I'll come with you."

"Don't be silly. One of us needs to stay dry. I'll hold on to the branches all the time so I don't get swept away."

The tree was growing on the bank, Jasmine reasoned, so its branches were part of the land, not the river. If she held on to them the whole time, she would always have contact with dry land, so she wouldn't really be in the river at all. It certainly wouldn't be dangerous.

She dropped the stick in the water and grabbed a handful of the spindly willow branches above her head.

"You can let go of my hand now," she said.

"Are you sure those branches will hold?"

Jasmine gave them a tug. "They're really strong. And I'm not *that* heavy. As soon as you let go, I'll grab another handful."

Tom let go. Jasmine grabbed at the branches and swung herself into the river. She gasped as her legs hit the freezing water. Grasping the branches, she tentatively tried to stand up.

Her feet sank into the mud and she gasped again as the water swirled around her waist. She continued to sink as she lowered her weight down. There didn't seem to be any solid bottom to the riverbed.

The only thing to do was to move along by grabbing on to branches, as though she was swinging along monkey bars.

Using this method, she moved steadily out into the river, getting closer and closer to the baby otter.

"Ow!" she cried, as her foot struck a sharp stone.

"What?" asked Tom. "Are you OK?"

"Fine," she said, wincing. "Just stubbed my toe."

She was really close now. She grabbed another branch, lifting her foot higher to avoid any more rocks. But when she lowered it again, there was no riverbed.

"I think it gets deep here," she said. "I can't touch the bottom any more."

A wave pushed the otter's body slightly towards her. She saw her chance. With her right hand, Jasmine reached out and grabbed the cub.

"Yes!" cried Tom. "You've got it!"

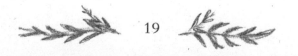

The baby otter wriggled in protest.

"It's moving!" said Tom in delight.

"Oh, no," gasped Jasmine, as the cub squirmed out of her grip. She was going to need both hands.

She let go of the branches and, frantically treading water, grasped the otter with one hand and worked its head clear of the branches with the other. Then she started to swim back.

It was really hard to keep the otter's head out of the water and make any progress. Jasmine panted and gasped with the effort, and found herself swallowing a mouthful of river water.

Coughing and spluttering, she finally reached the bank and stood up. The silt squished between her toes and the water swirled around her waist. Jasmine's teeth were chattering. The cub's eyes were closed. It was completely still.

"Hand it to me," said Tom. "Then you can climb up."

He clutched the tree root in one hand, leaned

over the edge of the bank and stretched his other hand down.

Jasmine held the cub as high as she could. Tom grasped it by the scruff of its neck, like a kitten.

"Got it," he said. "You can let go."

Jasmine let go. She scrabbled up the bank, clutching at plants and roots.

Tom laid the otter on Jasmine's jumper.

"It's shivering," he said. "It's freezing cold, poor thing."

"Dry it with my jumper," said Jasmine. "Then we can wrap it in yours once it's dry."

Tom rubbed the otter gently. "It's so cute," he said. "Look at its big paws. And it's got such thick fur."

Jasmine hauled herself up on to the flat ground. She was shivering, too.

"Rub it harder," she said. "Like Dad does with the new-born lambs. We need to warm it up fast. I'll do it while you take off your jumper."

Jasmine dried the baby otter's fur and then

they wrapped it in Tom's jumper. Tom picked up the little bundle and held it close to his chest as Jasmine wiped her feet on her wet jumper and pushed them into her wellies. She pulled her coat on and stuffed her socks into the pockets.

"Right," she said. "Let's take this baby home."

Chapter Four
An Incredible Find

"Mum!" called Jasmine, as she burst into the farmhouse just ahead of Tom.

"Hello!" called Nadia. They heard her study door open and she appeared at the top of the stairs.

"Mum, you'll never guess what we found!" said Jasmine. "Look!"

Nadia ran downstairs.

"Jasmine, you're soaking! What happened?"

"Look," said Jasmine. "It's amazing."

Tom opened his coat. Nadia's eyes grew wide

as she saw the sleeping otter wrapped in his jumper.

"An otter?" she breathed. "You found an otter cub? Where? How?"

"In the river," said Jasmine. "We heard it squawking, and we thought it was a bird's distress call, so we went down –" She stopped, remembering that her mother wouldn't approve. "I mean, we looked down, and we saw it, stranded on some stones. We waited for ages to see if its mum would come, but she didn't, and then a wave came and swept it into the river, and…" She glanced at Tom. How could she explain the next bit?

"Jasmine," said Nadia, in her sternest voice. "You didn't get into the river, did you?"

"I *had* to," protested Jasmine. "It was getting carried downstream and it couldn't swim against the current. I didn't jump in or anything," she added hastily, seeing her mum's horrified face. "It got caught in some willow branches, and I

reached in and got it."

Nadia shuddered. "I don't even want to think about it. But we'll deal with that later. Right now, we need to look after the otter."

She looked at the little cub and smiled.

"Well, aren't you beautiful?" She stroked the otter's head. Its fur was dry now and it looked so peaceful, snuggled in Tom's red jumper.

When Nadia looked up, her eyes were shining. "This is extraordinary, you know. There haven't been any otter cubs round here for years. Certainly not in my lifetime. What an incredible find."

"How should we look after it?" asked Jasmine.

"Well, I've never treated an otter, but the first step with any rescued animal is always rehydration. We don't know how long this little one has been away from its family. It might have been without fluids for some time. Can you mix up some rehydration formula, Jasmine?"

"Sure," Jasmine said. She started to squelch

towards the scullery, where Mum kept the medicines and equipment that she used in farm emergencies.

"Actually," said Mum, "you need to get changed first."

"I'm fine," said Jasmine.

"Don't be ridiculous. You're soaked to the skin. Go and put on some dry clothes. It'll only take you a minute."

Jasmine sighed and trudged upstairs. Sometimes, there was no point arguing with Mum.

"While Jasmine's changing," she heard Mum say to Tom, "you can weigh the otter. You'll need to keep a chart, like you did with Holly."

Holly was an abandoned kitten that Jasmine and Tom had rescued last winter. Nadia had shown them how to keep a chart recording her weight, feeding times and quantities, and every other aspect of her care and condition.

Jasmine changed quickly and hurried to the

scullery. The sleeping otter was lying in the scale pan while Tom wrote its weight on a notepad.

"Can you tell us if it's a boy or a girl?" asked Jasmine, as she took a new syringe and a sachet of rehydration formula from the cupboard.

Nadia lifted the cub off the scales, turned it on to its back and examined it.

"It's a female," she said.

"A girl," said Jasmine. "What shall we call her?"

"While you're thinking about that, I'll give her a quick health check," said Mum, "and you can get the formula ready. That water in the kettle should be about the right temperature."

Jasmine tipped the contents of the sachet into a measuring jug. Then she poured in the correct amount of cooled boiled water, and whisked the solution to dissolve the powder.

Nadia laid the otter on an old towel on the work surface, parting sections of fur to look at the skin.

"No wounds or bite marks," she said. "So she wasn't attacked."

"I can't believe how thick her fur is," said Jasmine.

"It keeps them warm in cold water," said
Mum. "Otters have two different layers of fur: a
short fluffy underfur, for warmth, and a longer
waterproof overfur, to keep them dry. But they're
not waterproof until about ten weeks, and I
would guess this one's younger than that. So it
would be able to float, but not swim yet. Their
mothers teach them to swim once their fur is
waterproof."

"So if we hadn't rescued her, she'd have
drowned," said Jasmine.

"Yes. Thank goodness you were there."

She examined each of the cub's big paws in
turn.

"Oh, she's got webbed feet!" said Tom.

"Sharp claws, too," said Jasmine.

Nadia turned her attention to the cub's ears.
"Otters have special flaps on their ears and nose,"
she said, "so they can close them when they
swim underwater. And their eyes work as well
underwater as they do on land."

She gently prised the cub's mouth open.

"Look, her teeth are beginning to come through. So I would guess she's still feeding mainly on her mother's milk, but also starting to eat fish."

"Should we give her fish?" asked Jasmine.

"For the moment, she just needs the rehydration formula. Is that the right temperature, Jasmine?"

Jasmine filled the syringe and dropped a little formula on to her wrist. The liquid felt the same temperature as her skin.

"It feels right to me," she said. "What do you think?"

Nadia held out her wrist and Jasmine dripped some formula on it.

"Perfect," she said.

"Can me and Tom feed her?" asked Jasmine.

"As long as you can get the fluid into her mouth properly. It's really important that it gets into her."

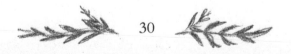

"I'll hold her," said Tom, "while you feed her."

They sat at the kitchen table and Nadia placed the sleeping otter, wrapped in the towel, on Tom's lap. Tom prised her jaws apart until Jasmine was able to slip the syringe's plastic nozzle into her mouth.

"Slow and steady," said Nadia. "Just dribble it in."

Jasmine drip-fed the fluid into the cub's mouth. The otter stayed completely still, her eyes closed.

After a few minutes, Nadia said, "You're doing a great job. Can you manage while I go and make some phone calls? I need to speak to an otter specialist to find out what to do once she's rehydrated."

"Sure," said Jasmine. "We'll be fine."

"I'll be in my study if you need me," said Mum.

A few seconds later, she appeared in the doorway again. "By the way," she said, "otters

have a ferocious bite. Even ones as small as this.
So if she starts to perk up, don't put your fingers
near her mouth. Try to keep her very calm and
quiet."

She left the room again. For several minutes,
Jasmine continued to drip-feed the fluid into the
otter's mouth.

"I wish she'd open her eyes," she said. "Or
twitch her nose, or do anything to show she's
getting better."

And just then, as if she had heard Jasmine's
wish, the cub lifted her head up. Her eyelids
flickered open and her perfectly round, bright
black eyes looked straight at Jasmine.

Chapter Five
Maybe We Can Keep Her

"Oh!" said Jasmine. "She's better!"

"She's so cute," said Tom, smiling as he stroked the otter's smooth fur.

"You're beautiful," said Jasmine to the cub. "I'm so happy you're better. I was so worried about you."

"What shall we call her?" said Tom.

Jasmine thought for a minute as she continued to feed the otter. "What about Splash?"

"Hmm," said Tom. He didn't sound convinced.

"River?"

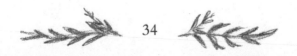

"River," repeated Tom, thoughtfully. "I'm not sure. She's a bit small to be called a whole river."

"Stream, then," said Jasmine. "Or Puddle."

Tom laughed. Then he said, "I know! What about Pebble? We found her among the pebbles, after all."

"Pebble," said Jasmine. "I like that. What do you think, little otter? How would you like to be called Pebble?"

The kitchen door opened and Mum appeared, holding the phone to her ear. Pebble turned towards the sound. Mum's face lit up in a delighted smile.

"Yes," she said to the person on the phone. "She's opened her eyes and started to look around. Yes, isn't it?"

She mouthed, "Well done," to the children and left the room again.

"We need to find her family," said Tom. "Once she's a bit better, we can go and look for them."

Jasmine's eyes lit up. "Imagine finding a whole

family of otters!"

"Can you believe this is the first otter cub around here for years and years?" said Tom. "We could be famous. The newspapers might come and take photos. We might be on TV."

"If she's an orphan," said Jasmine, "maybe we can keep her. Do people have pet otters?"

"I don't know," said Tom. "I don't know much about them, actually."

"Me neither," said Jasmine. "But we can find out."

When Mum returned, Pebble was sitting on Jasmine's lap, looking around curiously.

Tom had drawn up a very neat chart on a piece of paper and was filling in her

weight, time of feed and amount eaten.

"Oh, well done, you two," said Nadia. "She looks *so* much better!"

"Her name is Pebble," said Jasmine proudly. "What did the otter people say?"

"Well, I phoned Mira at the Wildlife Trust first," said Mum, "and she was *so* excited. They didn't think there were any breeding otters in Sussex. You're quite the local heroes."

"Will we be on TV?" asked Tom.

Mum laughed. "Definitely not, I'm afraid."

"Why not?" asked Jasmine, offended. "We'd be great on TV."

"I'm sure you would," said Mum, "but they don't want us to tell anyone about Pebble."

"Why not?" asked Tom.

"Well, imagine if you went on local television or radio and said you'd found an otter cub on this farm. What do you think would happen?"

"Loads of people would come here looking for otters?" said Tom.

"Yes, that's one thing. And otters are very shy. The last thing we want is to scare them away."

"What's the other thing?" asked Jasmine.

"Well," said Mum, "unfortunately, some people don't like otters."

"Don't like them? How could anybody not like otters?"

"Some fishermen don't like them because otters eat the fish they want to catch," said Mum. "It's hard to believe, but it was legal to hunt otters in this country until quite recently. That's one of the reasons why they almost became extinct."

"So if people knew there were otters here, they might come and hunt them?" asked Tom, horrified.

"It's possible," said Mum. "So there won't be any TV cameras here."

"What else did they say?" asked Jasmine.

"Well, they were concerned, of course, that this cub has been separated from her family. They

said you'd done the right thing to wait and see
if the mother came back. Once the cubs are this
age, the mother moves them between different
holts, and she carries them one at a time, so
she leaves one and comes back for it. That call
you heard is called a whistle. Cubs and mothers
communicate by whistling to each other."

"So Pebble was calling for her mother?"

"Probably," said Mum. "But since you waited
a long time and the mother didn't return, then
she might not have been moving her cubs. It's
possible that the holt was flooded and Pebble was
swept downstream."

"What did they say about looking after her?"
asked Jasmine.

"They gave me the number of an otter
specialist at Hemsley Wildlife Park, where they
rehabilitate a lot of cubs. He was very pleased
to hear that Pebble's already perking up, and he
said to continue rehydrating her for twenty-four
hours."

"And then do we start giving her milk?" asked Jasmine. "Or fish?"

"From what I told him about Pebble's weight and teeth, he reckons she's about eight weeks old," said Mum. "So they'll start her on a sort of fish soup, which is fish blended with milk."

"Wait a minute," said Jasmine. "What do you mean, 'they'?"

Nadia took a deep breath.

"Otters need expert care, Jasmine. Neil – that's the man I spoke to – said Pebble should be at a specialist centre where she can live with other otters."

Jasmine gaped in outrage. "What? No! We're looking after her. We're the ones who found her, not this Neil person."

"Otters aren't pets," said Mum. "They have to be handled properly and kept in the right conditions so they can be released back into the wild eventually. You want her to go back into the wild, don't you?"

"Of course," said Jasmine. "But we can look after her until then. We don't need some person called Neil butting in and taking her away from us."

"It's really important that she gets the right care as soon as possible," said Mum. "I don't just mean looking after her," she continued, as Jasmine opened her mouth to protest. "I know you and Tom are brilliant at looking after baby animals. But we don't want Pebble to imprint on you, do we?"

Jasmine knew about imprinting. If a baby animal is fed and handled by a human, it will think that person is its mother. And that means it will never be able to live in the wild again.

"Neil said she should go to a centre as soon as possible," said Mum, "so she can be with other otters and revert to her normal behaviour. The keepers at the wildlife park are too busy to fetch her themselves, so someone from the local Wildlife Rescue is coming to take her to the wildlife park tomorrow morning."

"Tomorrow?! No!" exclaimed Jasmine.

Pebble raised her head and squeaked in alarm.

"Sorry, Pebble," said Jasmine guiltily, stroking the back of the otter's sleek head.

"The sooner the better," said Mum, "if they're going to have the chance of rehabilitating her effectively."

"But then we'll hardly have any time with her."

"You've got until tomorrow morning," said Mum, "which is longer than most people ever have with an otter. Just think how lucky you are. The first otter cub to be spotted here in forty years, and you get to look after her for a whole night."

Jasmine said nothing. She couldn't believe they were going to have to say goodbye to Pebble so soon after finding her.

"I know it's hard," said Mum, "but you have to remember that she's not yours. She's a wild

creature and she belongs with others of her own kind. You've done an amazing job. She would almost certainly have died today if you and Tom hadn't rescued her. But you want the best for her, don't you? And I'm afraid that in this case, the best thing is to let her go."

Chapter Six
A Race Against Time

Jasmine was always prepared to argue her case until she exhausted her parents into submission. But, deep down, she knew it wouldn't be right to turn Pebble into a pet. She belonged in the wild, with other otters.

"At least you're sleeping over," she said to Tom. "We can do her night feeds."

Tom was staying at Jasmine's until Tuesday, while his parents were at a wedding. Tom hadn't been invited, for which he was very thankful.

"Pebble won't need night feeds," said Nadia.

"You can feed her at ten, and then get up at six for the early morning feed. And that's final," she said, as Jasmine opened her mouth to argue.

"What should she sleep in?" asked Tom.

"Neil said a big box lined with towels. Not cardboard, though, because she might try to chew through it."

"Sky's puppy crate?" Jasmine suggested. Sky was Jasmine's sheepdog.

"Good idea," said Mum. "Cover it with blankets. She'll be much calmer and less stressed in a dark place."

"It can go in my bedroom," said Jasmine.

Mum laughed. "With you and Tom chatting half the night? She needs peace and quiet."

"We'll be really quiet," Jasmine protested.

"No," said Mum. "You have to think about what's best for Pebble. She can go in Ella's room."

Ella was Jasmine's seventeen-year-old sister, and she was staying with a friend for the weekend.

Jasmine held Pebble while Mum and Tom carried the puppy crate up to Ella's room. Tom fetched a pile of old towels from the scullery and spread them over the floor of the crate.

"I'll make a hot water bottle in case she needs extra warmth," said Mum. "And Neil said they give the cubs a toy otter to keep them company."

Jasmine frowned in thought. She didn't have a toy otter.

"What about your toy cat?" asked Tom.

"Coco?" asked Jasmine.

"She's the same sort of colour and shape as an otter, and she's soft and furry."

"She might get ruined, though," said Mum. "I can put her in the washing machine afterwards, but she may never be the same again."

Jasmine stroked Pebble lovingly. "Coco won't mind," she said. "She'll be honoured to keep Pebble company."

"Put Pebble in the crate with her now, then,"

said Mum. "We should avoid handling Pebble as much as possible from now on, so she doesn't imprint."

Jasmine carried Pebble upstairs and carefully placed her in her new bed, while Tom closed the curtains. Pebble snuggled up next to the toy cat and closed her eyes.

"Oh, look," whispered Tom. "She likes Coco."

"You're our otter tonight, Pebble," Jasmine

murmured, as they draped blankets over the crate. "We're going to look after you. And tomorrow we'll find your home, so you can go back to your family."

As they ate their dinner at the kitchen table, Jasmine told her dad all about their exciting afternoon.

"I can't believe there are otters on this farm," he said. "That's fantastic."

"Amazing, isn't it?" said Mum.

"Where have you put the baby otter?" asked her little brother Manu. "I want to see it."

"You're not allowed anywhere near her," said Jasmine. "She needs peace and quiet."

"We'll be very quiet," said Manu. He turned to his friend. "Won't we, Ben?"

"Oh, my goodness, Manu, your hands are shocking," said Mum. "Go and wash them."

Ben slid his hands under the table.

"I already washed them," said Manu.

"Wash them again, please. You too, Ben. And use the nailbrush. Your fingernails are full of dirt. What have you been doing?"

"We're digging for treasure," said Manu as he and Ben went over to the sink.

"With your hands?"

"The earth's really soft. And you can feel stuff better with your hands."

"We're looking for Roman remains," said Ben.

"Did you find any?" asked Dad.

"We're not sure," said Manu. "We found some stuff that might be Roman. We're going to look again after dinner."

"I wonder where the holt is," said Dad.

"What's a holt?" asked Manu.

"An otter's home," said Mum. "Which reminds me, Jasmine. The Wildlife Trust people are keen to reunite Pebble with her family if possible. If the landowners give permission, they're planning to look along the riverbanks tomorrow, on our land and on the neighbouring farms where the river runs through them."

"But we're going to do that," said Jasmine. "It's our farm and we're the ones who found Pebble."

"You can look as well," said Mum. "There's a lot of riverbank, and it's not a competition."

Oh, yes, it is, thought Jasmine.

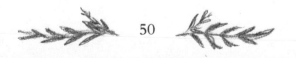

"We'll find it first," Tom whispered.

"Anyway," said Mum, "you should be warned that, according to Neil, it's extremely unlikely we'll ever find Pebble's family."

"Oh, well, *Neil* would say that, wouldn't he?" said Jasmine. "He just wants to keep Pebble for himself."

Mum gave her a stern look.

"Jasmine, just listen, please, before you take a dislike to somebody you've never met. Neil has been rehabilitating otters for years, so he knows what he's talking about."

Jasmine made a face, but she said nothing.

"It's very unlikely that you'd see an actual otter," said Mum. "They're highly solitary, and they rarely come out during the day. You can look for tracks and signs, but it's still very difficult to locate the family, because the mother moves her cubs around a lot. Her territory might be fourteen kilometres of river, and the river only goes through our land for a few kilometres."

"So they might not even be on this farm," said Tom, looking worried. "But what will happen to Pebble if we don't find them?"

"She'll stay at the wildlife park for a year or so, until she's old enough to be released. Then they'll release her as close as possible to where she was found. She'll need to be released near other otters, so they know it's a good habitat, but not in a place where an adult male otter is living."

"Why not?" asked Jasmine.

"Well, apparently he would harm a young one on his territory."

"But how would they know if there was an adult male living there? You just said it's really hard to see otters. So they might release her and then she'd get attacked."

"Please may we leave the table?" asked Manu.

"If you're finished," said Mum. "Have you had enough to eat, Ben?"

"Yes, thank you," said Ben. "Thank you for the

lovely dinner, Nadia."

Ben was always extremely polite to adults. That was how he got away with being so naughty.

"So we need to make sure we find Pebble's family," said Tom.

"Definitely," said Jasmine. "I won't let her be brought up in an orphanage and then let loose to get mauled."

"One more thing," said Mum. "Neil said even if the mother is found, there's not much chance she'll take the cub back if they've been apart for more than forty-eight hours."

"So we've only got until Sunday afternoon," said Tom.

"Please can we borrow your laptop after dinner, Mum?" asked Jasmine. "We need to do some research."

This is a race against time, she thought. *And we're going to win it.*

Chapter Seven

What Have You Done With Her?

"Let's check on Pebble before we start researching," said Tom as they went upstairs after dinner.

"We'll just creep in and peep under the blanket," said Jasmine. "She's probably sleeping."

They tiptoed in at the open door of Ella's room. Which was odd, thought Jasmine, because she was sure they'd closed the door when they left the room.

The blankets were draped messily over the puppy crate. This was also odd. Jasmine could

have sworn they'd done a neater job than that.

They knelt in front of the crate and Jasmine lifted a corner of the blanket. She couldn't see Pebble. She lifted the blanket higher.

The toy cat was there. The hot water bottle was there. But Pebble was nowhere to be seen.

Jasmine and Tom gasped. Then they sprang to their feet.

"Manu!" yelled Jasmine, racing out of the room.

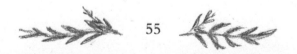

Tom grabbed her arm. "Shh. If he's got Pebble, we don't want to frighten her."

"Of course he's got Pebble," spat Jasmine. "I'm going to kill him. I'm going to actually kill him."

"OWWW!!"

A howl of pain came from Manu's room. Jasmine and Tom rushed in.

Ben was hopping around the room, his face screwed up in agony, sucking his index finger. Manu's feet were sticking out from under the bed.

"Where's Pebble?" demanded Jasmine.

"She bit me!" said Ben. "She bit me really hard."

"Good," said Jasmine. "You deserved it. Where is she? What have you done with her?"

"She's somewhere under here," said Manu from under the bed. "She ran away after she bit Ben."

"Get out from there right now, you idiot!" hissed Jasmine, kneeling down and tugging

Manu's ankles.

"Ow! Get off me! I'm coming out."

"Stop shouting," said Tom. "You'll scare her even more."

"Ugh, there's a wet patch," squealed Manu, as he squirmed out from under the bed. "Oh, yuck, it's weed on my carpet. Ugh, I'm covered in otter wee."

"Serves you right," said Jasmine, pushing him aside and wriggling under the bed. "Get out."

It was dim and dusty under Manu's bed, and there wasn't much room to move between the boxes of Lego and broken toys. Jasmine heard Tom telling the boys to leave, and then there was silence. She lay still and listened.

After a while, she heard a scuffling noise from the far corner. She turned towards the noise and saw a bright little eye looking back at her from behind a plastic digger.

Jasmine was about to grab Pebble when she

realised what a bad idea that was. Pebble must be terrified. She would probably bite any hand that came near her. Jasmine needed to cover her with a cloth to calm her down before she caught her.

"Tom," Jasmine whispered.

"Yes?"

"Can you get a blanket?"

Tom left the room. Pebble didn't move.

Jasmine prayed that the otter would be all right. What if she was injured?

She heard Tom come back.

"Here you go," he whispered, pushing the blanket under the bed.

Keeping her hands behind the fabric, Jasmine held out the blanket and inched closer to the little cub. Once she was within reach, she slowly lifted the blanket as high as she could and dropped it over Pebble. Then she grasped her round her middle. Holding the bundle firmly in both hands, she wriggled out from under the bed.

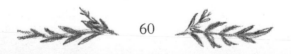

"Well done," whispered Tom, as Jasmine carried Pebble into Ella's room. She lowered the otter into the crate, next to the toy cat. Only then did she remove the blanket.

Pebble sat on the towels, looking around. They could see her ribs heaving up and down beneath her fur.

"You poor little thing," said Jasmine. "What a horrible shock. Are you all right?"

Several sets of footsteps came running up the stairs. Mum appeared in the doorway.

"Oh, good, you've got her back," she whispered.

Manu peered into the room. Ben lurked behind him.

"Come on, Tom," said Jasmine, covering the crate with the blanket and walking out on to the landing. She wanted Manu to get a proper telling off, but Pebble needed peace and quiet.

"That otter is vicious," said Manu. "It nearly bit Ben's finger off."

"Why on earth was Ben putting his finger in her mouth?" asked Mum.

"He was trying to feed her."

"Feed her what?"

"Crisps," said Manu.

"Crisps!"

"We thought she'd like them. Otters eat fish, don't they?"

"Crisps aren't fish, Manu."

"These were. They were prawn cocktail crisps."

"How could you be so stupid?" said Mum. "She's a wild animal, and she's just lost her family. What were you thinking, to take her out of her bed and treat her like a toy?"

"It's not fair," said Manu. "Jasmine gets all the animals. We just wanted one for us."

"Well, the way you've just behaved with this one, it will be a very long time before you ever get one of your own."

"Like *never*," said Jasmine. "Can't you get him adopted, Mum? This family would be so much

better without him."

"Don't be ridiculous," said Mum. "Who on earth do you think would adopt Manu? Now, let's clean up this bite, Ben."

"Yes, Nadia," said Ben. "Thank you, Nadia."

"And don't even think about going into Ella's room again, Manu," said Mum, "or this will be the last sleepover you ever have."

Chapter Eight
We Promise

Once everyone had calmed down, Jasmine and Tom tiptoed into Ella's room.

Jasmine lifted a corner of the blanket and peered into the crate.

"Pebble's sleeping," she whispered.

Tom crouched beside her. "She looks all right, don't you think?"

"She'd better be," said Jasmine, "or I'll never speak to Manu again."

Back in Jasmine's room, they sat on the bed and researched otters on Nadia's laptop, while

Jasmine groomed Marmite, her black cat, who was sitting on her lap. Marmite's brother, Toffee, lay curled up next to Jasmine.

"It says otters usually have two or three cubs at a time," said Tom. "So Pebble probably has brothers or sisters. They must be missing her, too."

"If they're anything like my brother," said Jasmine, "she's probably glad to be away from them."

"Otters and badgers have five toes, but dogs and foxes only have four," said Tom. "That should help with identifying footprints."

Jasmine studied the photographs of muddy footprints on the screen.

"Otter and badger prints look almost the same," she said. "It says the badger ones have

longer claws, but I can't see any difference."

"Mink footprints are similar, too," said Tom, pointing them out, "but they're smaller. It says you can cover a mink print with a two-pound coin. We should take one with us."

"Let's make a list of what to take," said Jasmine. "Sorry, Marmite. I need to get up."

She lifted the cat off her lap and fetched a notebook and pen from her desk. At the top of a clean page, she wrote: *Otter Spotters List*.

"There's drawings of all different animal prints here, actual size," said Tom. "Let's print the page and take it with us."

Jasmine added it to the list.

"And we should take binoculars," said Tom. "It says you can often spot the entrance holes to a holt better from the opposite side of the river. Do you have binoculars?"

"Only plastic ones," said Jasmine, "but we can borrow Dad's." She wrote it on the list.

"Otters are nocturnal," said Tom, "so dusk and

66

dawn are the best times to see them. They lie up and rest during the day. It says early morning is best. But we should stay away from the water's edge. If you go too close to the water, it stresses them. And we need to look out for muddy slopes on the bank. Otters use them as chutes to slide into the water."

"Anything else?"

"Don't wear perfume. They'll pick up the scent."

Jasmine laughed. "As if we'd wear perfume!"

"And we should take silver foil," said Tom, "for bringing home otter droppings."

"Why would we bring them home?"

"I guess so we can show them to the experts, to check if they really are from otters."

"What do otter droppings look like?"

"There's a picture here," said Tom. "They're called spraints."

Jasmine looked at the screen, which showed two close-up photos. One was labelled "Fresh

Otter Spraint" and the other one "Old Otter Spraint".

"It says you should smell droppings to check if they're otter spraint," said Tom. He read on and laughed.

"What?" said Jasmine.

"It says, 'Otter spraint smells almost pleasantly fishy, with a hint of jasmine tea.' So maybe it smells a bit like you!"

"Oh, ha ha," said Jasmine.

"They use their spraint to mark their territory," said Tom, "so we should look in noticeable places, like on top of big rocks and tree roots by the river."

"And we should also look for fish heads and crayfish claws," said Jasmine. "It says they leave them behind after they've eaten."

Tom laughed. "So we're going to spend tomorrow staring at mud, sniffing poo and looking for bits of dead river creatures. Nice."

Pebble didn't seem to have suffered any
permanent damage from her ordeal. She drank
all the rehydration formula at her ten o'clock
feed, and again at six o'clock on Saturday
morning. When they put her back in her crate,
she scampered to the side and looked out at
them with her bright, intelligent eyes.

"Ella will be sorry to have missed her," said
Mum. "You know how much she loves cute
baby animals."

"I wish she didn't have to go," said Jasmine.

"She's well hydrated now," said Mum. "She's
ready to travel to the centre. Neil said they
usually get a lot more lively once they're with
other otters."

"Anyway, she'll only be gone for a day or two,"
said Tom. "As soon as we find her family, she can
come back."

"When you go shopping today, Mum," Jasmine
said as they were eating their breakfast, "could

you buy jasmine tea, please?"

"Whatever for?" asked Mum.

"To see if it smells like otter droppings."

"Sounds delicious. I can't wait to try it."

"You've caused a lot of excitement with your find," said Dad. "There's a couple of people from the Wildlife Trust scouring the riverbank for otters. Mum's friend Mira and somebody else."

"See?" said Jasmine, rounding on Nadia. "I told you we should have gone out earlier. Now they'll find Pebble's home and we won't get to do anything."

Nadia sighed. "Does it matter who finds Pebble's home? The only thing that matters is finding it, surely. Anyway, you had to feed your animals and walk Sky first. And I thought you wanted to be here when the woman from the Wildlife Rescue comes to collect Pebble."

"Me and Ben are going to look for otters, too," said Manu. "I bet we'll find them first."

"You and Ben aren't going anywhere near the

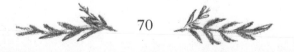

70

river," said Jasmine. "Tell him, Mum. They'd scare away all the wildlife for miles around."

Mum was about to speak when the doorbell rang. Jasmine and Tom followed her out to the hall.

Mum opened the door to reveal a tall, thin woman holding a wooden crate with several round holes in the top.

"Good morning," she said. "I'm Prunella Sharp. I've come to collect the otter cub."

"Come in," said Mum. "Thank you so much for doing this."

Prunella Sharp stepped into the hall.

"This is Jasmine and Tom," said Mum. "They found the otter."

Prunella Sharp gave them a sweeping up-and-down glance. She didn't seem impressed.

"Jasmine and Tom are going to look for the holt today," said Mum. "Neil said we need to find it as quickly as possible if we want the mother to accept Pebble back."

The woman gave them a pitying smile.

"I'm afraid the chances of your being able to reintroduce this cub to its family are practically

non-existent. The female's territory could be up to fourteen kilometres long, and otters move about all the time, so there'll be several holts. You'll have no way of knowing which one she's actually using. It's really not worth wasting your time."

"That's not a very good attitude," said Jasmine. "It's got to be worth a try, surely?"

Mum gave Jasmine a warning look, which Jasmine pretended not to see.

"Also," said Prunella Sharp, shooting a poisonous look at Jasmine, "it's very possible that the mother rejected this cub. They do that quite often, unfortunately. And in that case, she certainly wouldn't take her back."

She pulled a pair of thick gloves out of her handbag.

"Where is the cub? I need to get on. It's a long journey."

"Of course," said Mum. "She's upstairs."

Jasmine and Tom followed them up to Ella's

room. Mum opened the puppy crate. The woman put her gloves on and grabbed Pebble by the scruff of her neck. Pebble growled and bared her teeth.

Please bite her, Jasmine begged silently. *Give her a really hard nip right through those gloves.*

Pebble kept her teeth bared and continued to growl as she wriggled and squirmed in the woman's grasp. To Jasmine's disappointment, Prunella Sharp managed to lower her into the carrying crate without getting bitten. She shut the lid.

"Wait!" said Jasmine.

She went to the puppy crate and fished out the toy cat. "This is Coco. Pebble needs her to keep her company on the journey."

Prunella Sharp took the toy without a word and put it in the case. Then she closed the lid and snapped the clasps shut.

"Goodbye, Pebble," said Tom, through the holes in the box. "We'll see you again very soon."

"Goodbye, Pebble," said Jasmine. "We're going out right now to find your family. And we won't stop until we've found them. We promise."

Chapter Nine
The Otter Spotters

By half past five that afternoon, Tom and Jasmine were weary and fed up. They had sniffed a lot of droppings, none of which smelled pleasantly fishy with a hint of jasmine tea. They had found a lot of footprints, all of which, on close inspection, turned out to have been made by dogs or foxes. And, since they had eaten their packed lunches at ten thirty in the morning, they were also very hungry.

"It's hopeless," said Jasmine. "We're never going to find anything. Cruella Sharp was right."

"She only said the chances were *practically* non-existent," said Tom. "She didn't say they were *totally* non-existent. So even she admitted we've got a chance."

Jasmine grabbed his arm. "Look!"

"What?"

She pointed across the river. "Do you see that hole in the bank?"

They stared at the opposite bank. "It's got all the right things for a holt," said Jasmine. "It's muddy, and there's a big old tree stump and a fallen branch at the top of the bank."

"Let's investigate," said Tom.

Fired up with excitement, they ran back to the bridge and hurried along the opposite riverbank until they reached the tree stump. Its lumpy roots protruded from the ground like the toes of some gnarled old giant.

"We should be really quiet," Jasmine murmured. "If this is where Pebble's family are living, we don't want to scare them away."

They started to search the muddy
ground around the tree roots. After
a few minutes, Tom whispered,
"Jasmine! Footprints!"

He was staring at a patch of bare mud
under an oak tree a little way away from
the tree stump. Jasmine hurried across and
crouched beside him.

"Five toes," she whispered. "Definitely
bigger than a two-pound coin."

"Could be a badger, though," said
Tom.

He rummaged in his rucksack and
took out the crumpled piece of paper
with the life-size drawings of animal
prints on it.

"What do you think?" he asked.

"Ow!" said Jasmine.

Something hard had hit her on the head.
She rubbed the sore spot and looked on

the ground where the object
had fallen. It was a little green
acorn.

She looked at the drawings again,
and then at the footprints. She turned
to Tom and grinned.

"I think they're otter prints," she
whispered.

"Me too! I'll take some photos."

"There should be spraint somewhere,"
said Jasmine. "I'll look."

As she crouched under the tree,
another hard object hit her on
the head. Jasmine stared
at the green acorn as it
fell on the ground.

"Why are acorns falling?
They're not even ripe."

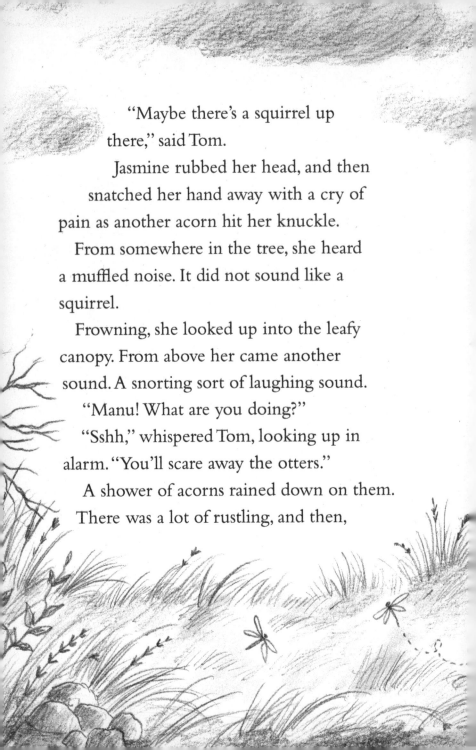

"Maybe there's a squirrel up there," said Tom.

Jasmine rubbed her head, and then snatched her hand away with a cry of pain as another acorn hit her knuckle.

From somewhere in the tree, she heard a muffled noise. It did not sound like a squirrel.

Frowning, she looked up into the leafy canopy. From above her came another sound. A snorting sort of laughing sound.

"Manu! What are you doing?"

"Sshh," whispered Tom, looking up in alarm. "You'll scare away the otters."

A shower of acorns rained down on them. There was a lot of rustling, and then,

framed in oak leaves,
appeared the grinning
faces of Manu and Ben.

Jasmine just about managed
to stop herself from shouting.

"You idiots," she hissed.
"There's an otter
holt here and you're
going to scare them
all away."

"Those aren't otter footprints," said Manu. "They're badgers'."

"How would you know? They're otter prints."

"No, they're not."

"Yes, they are."

"Be quiet, you two," said Tom, in a furious whisper.

"I'm not even talking to you, anyway," Jasmine said to Manu. "We've got important work to do."

"Important work looking for the wrong animal," said Manu.

Ben laughed. Jasmine made a face at them and turned back to her search. She was even more determined now to find some otter spraint.

They worked in silence for a while, trying to ignore the whispering and muffled laughter from above them. Then the leaves rustled again and Manu's face appeared.

"You can ask Dad if you like," he said. "Look, he's over there." He cupped his hands around his mouth and yelled, "DAD! DAD! Over here!"

Tom gave Jasmine a look of despair. "Great," he said. "That should really help."

"Thanks, Manu," said Jasmine. "You are literally the worst brother in the history of the universe."

"How are you getting on?" called Jasmine's dad, who was walking across the field carrying a fresh mineral block for the sheep.

"Well, we *were* getting on really well," said Jasmine, scowling into the tree, "until they decided to ruin everything again."

"We think we've found otter footprints," said Tom, pointing to the muddy tracks. "I've taken photos. And there's a hole in the side of the bank down there that looks like the entrance to a holt."

"We think this is Pebble's home," said Jasmine. "So we can phone the wildlife centre and they can bring her back."

Dad was crouching over the footprints. "I'm sorry to bring bad news," he said, "but these look

like badger prints to me."

"Told you!" said Manu.

Jasmine looked at her father in dismay. "But otter and badger prints look almost the same. How do you know they're not otters?"

"Well, I've seen a lot of badger prints over the years," said Dad, "and these look like badger to me."

"But—" Jasmine began.

"More importantly, though," he said, "there's a badger sett right over there, and the badgers hunt in this field at night."

He indicated the steep hedgerow bank at the edge of the field, in front of a patch of woodland. There were several large holes in the side of the bank.

"Can you see a path worn in the grass from these footprints to those holes?" asked Dad.

They looked. Sure enough, Jasmine saw a faint narrow path where the grass had been trodden down.

"That's where they come out to look for food," said Dad.

"Told you," said Manu again.

"Shut up, Manu," said Jasmine.

"How did you know, anyway?" Tom asked Manu.

"I just know stuff," said Manu.

Dad smiled. "I showed him the sett and all the signs to look for when he was building a den over there."

Jasmine heaved a huge sigh. She felt as flat as a burst balloon.

Dad squeezed her shoulder. "Cheer up, Jasmine. It's incredibly hard to spot an otter. I've never seen one and I've lived here all my life."

"How is that meant to cheer me up?" demanded Jasmine. "If we don't find Pebble's family by tomorrow, then she'll have to stay at the wildlife centre until she's grown up, and she'll never see her mum again." She was close to tears now. "And what about her family?

They won't know where she is and they'll be so worried about her."

Dad gave her a hug. "You must be exhausted, Jas. Come in for tea. You'll feel a lot better once you've had something to eat."

Jasmine looked at Tom. "Do you want to go in for tea?"

Tom looked as downcast as Jasmine felt. "Sure," he said. "We're more likely to see otters at dusk, anyway."

"We'll come out again after tea," said Jasmine, "and we'll stay out until dark. We have to find Pebble's family. They must be around here somewhere."

Chapter Ten
Just This Once

Jasmine poured onion gravy over her sausages and mash.

"Did you get the jasmine tea, Mum?" she asked.

"I didn't, I'm afraid," said Mum.

"Why not?"

"Because," said Mum, "I had a lot of things to do this morning, and I really didn't have time to search the health food shop for tea that smells like otter poo. I do have some potentially exciting news about the otters, though."

"What's that?" asked Jasmine.

"The people from the Wildlife Trust have found otter spraint and tracks on Ivor Cornwell's farm. Mira's setting up an infra-red camera there tonight."

"Oh," said Jasmine. She knew she should be pleased, but what she felt was disappointment. It should have been her and Tom who found the holt.

"She asked if you'd like to go with her," said Mum. "She's planning to stay there for an hour or so before it gets dark, in case she can spot any otters."

"Oh, yes, please!" said Tom, his eyes sparkling.

"Is Mira nice?" asked Jasmine. "She's not like Prunella Sharp, is she?"

Mum smiled. "She's very nice. And not at all like Prunella Sharp."

"Thank you for taking us," said Tom, as he and Jasmine climbed into the back seat of

Mira's truck.

"Not at all," said Mira. "You were the ones who found the otter, after all."

The sun was beginning to set as they drove along the village lane, through a gateway and across a couple of Ivor Cornwell's fields. Mira parked the truck in another gateway and they walked to a clump of trees several metres back from the river.

"We'll be screened here," she said, "but we've got a good view of the bank. And we're upwind of the river, so our scent won't get carried on the breeze." She spread out a rug. "Sit down and make yourselves comfortable."

She pointed out a tree stump close to the river. "That's where we found the spraint, and there were tracks leading from it to the water."

"Were they definitely otter tracks?" asked Jasmine.

"We're as sure as we can be," said Mira. "But the otter might not be Pebble's mother. It could

 89

easily be a lone male. And it may not show up
again tonight, because it might have moved on
to another holt. The camera will tell us if any
otters do visit."

From her rucksack she took a brick-shaped
object, covered in a camouflage
pattern. It had a small round lens
in the centre and a long strap
attached to the back.

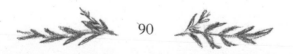

"It's camouflaged so
animals won't spot it," she
said. "And it's completely
silent."

"Isn't it really boring
watching the film afterwards?"
asked Jasmine. "Just staring at a picture of a
riverbank, with nothing going on?"

Mira smiled. "It's a clever camera. It's motion-
sensitive. So it only starts filming when
something walks in front of the lens. It's timed to
film for one minute, but if the animal's still there

after a minute, it will take another one-minute
film, and so on."

"That's so cool," said Jasmine.

"Where are you going to put it?" asked Tom.

"I'll strap it to the bottom of that tree trunk,"
said Mira, pointing to a young silver birch.
"And I'll put a brick in front of it for sprainting.
Otters almost always leave a spraint wherever
they go, and if you provide a brick, they'll use it.
So if they do come, we should get some good
footage."

She strapped the camera to the tree trunk and
placed the brick in front of it. Then she joined
Tom and Jasmine on the rug.

The sun was going down in a blaze of orange
light. On the riverbank, nothing moved except
the leaves in the breeze.

Then Jasmine heard a rustling sound in the
grass.

She glanced at Tom. It was clear from his
excited expression that he'd heard it too. All

three pairs of eyes scrutinised the place where the sound had come from.

The rustling continued. Something snuffled. Jasmine strained her eyes to see, but the long grass hid whatever animal was making the sounds.

The sounds stopped.

They waited.

The rustling and snuffling started again. And then an animal emerged. An animal with a stripy black-and-white face and a long snout.

It was great to see a badger, of course. But it wasn't an otter. And when the last traces of light finally vanished from the sky, they had still seen no sign of Pebble's family.

"Don't despair," said Mira, as they trudged through the darkness back to the truck. "Hopefully the camera will show some otter activity tonight."

"And hopefully it will be Pebble's family," said Tom. "Then Pebble could come back tomorrow."

Chapter Eleven
A Little Phone Call

Just before nine the following morning,
Jasmine and Tom walked along the lane to Ivor
Cornwell's farm. Mira was coming back at nine
o'clock to look at the camera footage, and they
wanted to be there to see it.

As they drew near to the gateway, though,
Mira drove out of the field. She waved and
stopped the truck on the verge.

"Hello, you two," she said, as she opened the
driver's door and jumped down on to the grass.

"You're early," said Jasmine.

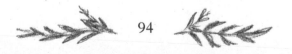

"Yes. I was on my way to see you."

"Did any otters come?" asked Tom.

Mira shook her head. "I'm really sorry."

"No otters at all?" asked Jasmine.

"Sadly not. Just that badger, and a fox early this morning. We've had other volunteers out looking since dawn, and they've found nothing either. Otters are extremely hard to find, I'm afraid. They'll return to that holt at some point, but maybe not for a couple of weeks."

"Pebble's family won't take her back in two weeks' time," said Jasmine.

"At least you saved Pebble's life," said Mira. "You can be very proud of that."

"But we haven't found her family. She'll have to live in an orphanage. And when she gets released, she'll be all alone in the world."

"She'll be an adult by then," said Mira, "and otters are solitary creatures. They always live alone, except when they have cubs."

"Exactly," said Jasmine. "Except when they

have cubs. Pebble's mum must be so worried."

"I'm very sorry," said Mira. "Can I at least give you a lift home?"

"Oh, look," said Tom, nudging Jasmine. "It's Mrs Thomas."

An old lady in wellies and a tweed skirt was walking along the lane towards them. She smiled and waved at the children.

"It's OK, thank you," said Jasmine to Mira. "We're going to keep on looking."

Mira said again how sorry she was, and then, with a wave, she drove off.

"How nice to see you both," said Mrs Thomas. "How are you?"

Her kind face made Jasmine feel a little bit better. Mrs Thomas was one of the nicest people she knew.

"Fine, thank you," she said. "How's Willow?"

Willow was a baby goat that Tom and Jasmine had rescued earlier in the summer. She now lived with Mrs Thomas as a companion for her elderly goat, Bluebell.

"Willow's wonderful," said Mrs Thomas. "Come back with me and see her, if you like."

"We'd love to," said Jasmine, "but we have to hunt for otters."

They told her about Pebble and the search for her family. "So, you see, we need to look along the riverbank again," said Tom.

"Well, why don't you come for tea later?" said Mrs Thomas. "I'll make you that chocolate cake you like. And Willow would love to see you."

"We'd love to see her, too," said Jasmine. "Thank you so much."

97

Mrs Thomas lived in a small cottage with a big garden. Tom and Jasmine traipsed wearily up the drive after another fruitless day's otter spotting.

As they walked around the side of the house towards the paddock, they heard a high-pitched bleat. Their dejected faces broke into smiles as Willow bounded towards them, leaping through an old tyre that they had hung from a tree for her to play on.

"Wow, Willow, you're getting even more agile," said Jasmine. "We're going to have to make you some more things for your obstacle course."

Mrs Thomas came out of her back door as they were climbing over the gate into the paddock. Jasmine scooped Willow into her arms and Tom took a carrot out of his rucksack. Willow grabbed it between her teeth.

"Manners, Willow," said Mrs Thomas, laughing. She stroked Bluebell, who had trotted across the field at a more sedate pace. Tom gave her a carrot, too. They had stocked up with goat treats from the farmhouse fridge at lunchtime.

After they had played with Willow, Mrs Thomas gave them a delicious tea of sandwiches, scones, biscuits and, of course, her special chocolate cake. While they ate, Tom and Jasmine updated her on their search for Pebble's family.

"We've looked right along the riverbank on our farm," said Jasmine, "and the Wildlife Trust people have searched Ivor Cornwell's farm, too,

and Roger Turner's."

Mrs Thomas suddenly looked alert.

"I bet they haven't searched Angus Mizon's land, have they?"

"Who's Angus Mizon?" asked Jasmine.

"He owns the land on either side of mine," said Mrs Thomas. "The river runs under the road at the edge of your farm, and then right across his land."

"So we need to search his bit of river," said Jasmine. "Pebble's family might have moved to a holt there."

"The problem is," said Mrs Thomas, "he won't let anyone on his farm. He fell out with the Wildlife Trust years ago and he won't let them set foot on the place."

"Why?" asked Tom.

"Goodness knows," said Mrs Thomas. "He's a miserable old so-and-so. Falls out with everyone."

"Then we'll just sneak in," said Jasmine. "He

won't even see us."

"Unfortunately," said Mrs Thomas, "his house is at the top of a slope, with an excellent view of the river. He keeps a pretty close eye on it. He's caught people fishing without permission a couple of times, and he has no hesitation in reporting them to the police."

"So it's useless, then," said Tom.

Mrs Thomas looked thoughtful. "I'm not sure. He owes me a favour, and he doesn't want to get on the wrong side of me."

"How come?" asked Tom.

"That road," said Mrs Thomas, pointing out of the window to the rough track that ran past the back of her house. "It belongs to me, but I let him use it. Otherwise he'd have to drive out on to the main road and then back on to his land every time he needed to get from one field to another. So I signed an agreement saying he can drive across my land. But I can cancel the agreement whenever I want to."

She set down her teacup and stood up. "Perhaps a little phone call is in order. What do you think?"

Jasmine and Tom waited anxiously for Mrs Thomas to return. But when she came back in, she was smiling.

"That's settled, then," she said.

"Really?" said Jasmine. "We can look for otters on his land?"

"He wasn't very happy about it. He dislikes children even more than fishermen and dog walkers. But I explained that it was an emergency, and you only need to look on his land because you're trying to reunite Pebble with her family. After a lot of mumbling and grumbling, he agreed, as long as you understood it was just this once. He said if he ever sees you there again, he'll go straight to the police."

Chapter Twelve
A Perfect Place for Otters

"If I was an otter," said Tom, "this is where I'd live."

It was a particularly beautiful stretch of river. The banks were thick with reeds and flowers. Fish swam just below the surface. A mallard duck sailed serenely through the water, five fluffy ducklings bobbing behind her.

After walking for an hour through fields of sheep and cows, they came to a wooden bridge. Just beyond the bridge was a bend in the river. A wire fence marked the edge of the field.

"This must be the end of Angus Mizon's land," said Jasmine. "Mrs Thomas said his farm ended at the field with the bridge, didn't she? Let's cross over and walk back along the other side."

"Doesn't that look a perfect place for otters?" said Tom, pointing to the opposite bank.

Across the river was a big tree stump and a pile of logs, where a tree had been felled and the trunk sawn into smaller pieces. Bright green moss grew over the logs, so they had obviously been there for some time.

"But we've seen so many good places," said Jasmine, "and no otters in any of them."

Just then, she saw something else on the bank below the logs.

"Look!" she said. "A mud slide!"

Tom's eyes grew very wide. Then he started to run. Jasmine grabbed his arm.

"We need to be quiet," she whispered.

They tiptoed across the bridge and over to the patch of bare mud leading down to the water.

They crouched beside it.

Jasmine sighed. "No footprints. Completely bare."

"That doesn't mean there haven't been otters here, though," said Tom. "If they were here before all that rain, their footprints will have been washed away."

"Let's look for other signs," said Jasmine.

They worked in silence for several minutes. Then Jasmine let out a cry of excitement. She clamped her hand over her mouth, horrified at the noise she'd made.

"Tom!" she whispered, but there was no need. He was already beside her.

"Wow," he said. "That's amazing."

They stared in delight at the top of a wet log covered in lichen. Scattered over the log were the little white bones of what had almost definitely once been a fish.

They grinned at each other. A real sign at last!

Tom took photos of the bones while Jasmine

hunted for more evidence, her heart beating fast.

"These bones look quite old, don't you think?" said Tom. "If they're two weeks' old, the otters might be due to come back here."

He put his camera away and started scrutinising the roots around the tree stump. After a few minutes, he whispered, "Jasmine, look at this."

Jasmine looked. Tom was staring at a little pile of crumbly, greenish-white remains.

"Do you think that might be spraint?" he asked.

"We need to inspect it," said Jasmine. "Where's the silver foil?"

Tom found the foil and smoothed it out on the ground. Using two small twigs, Jasmine picked up a piece of the crumbly stuff and dropped it on the foil. Then she bent down and sniffed.

"Ugh," she said, straightening up again. "That definitely smells fishy."

"Pleasantly fishy, with a hint of jasmine tea?" asked Tom.

"Well, we'll never know about the jasmine tea," said Jasmine, "since my mum was so mean about buying it."

She poked it. "These could definitely be fish bones and scales. We might have actually found a holt!"

"And all these things have been here for a while," said Tom. "Which means the otters might come back tonight."

"Imagine if we see Pebble's family swimming down the river!" said Jasmine.

"Let's watch from the bridge," said Tom. "Then we'll have a good view in both directions."

They leaned on the railings of the bridge, looking hopefully at the river, until the sun began to sink over the hills.

"We should phone your mum," said Tom. "We promised we'd be home before dark, and she's going to walk Sky to the main road to

meet us, isn't she?"

Jasmine sighed. "I guess so. We'll just have to come back really early tomorrow."

Tom looked worried. "But he said we could only come just this once."

"It *is* just this once. It's all part of the same thing."

"I bet he won't think so," said Tom.

He paused. Then he said, "It's already more than forty-eight hours since we found Pebble. It might be too late for her family to take her back."

Jasmine looked at him, outraged. "What are you saying? You think we should give up now,

when we've found a holt they might come to tonight? Are you crazy?"

"But what if he catches us in the morning and calls the police?"

"He'll never catch us. We'll come really early, before he's even up. Anyway, he's not going to be looking out for us, is he?"

But as they walked back across the field, a light came on in an upstairs window of Angus Mizon's house. At the window, they saw a man lift a pair of binoculars to his eyes.

"He's watching us," hissed Jasmine.

They kept their heads down and quickened their pace. The binocular lenses glinted in the light of the setting sun.

"I don't like this," said Tom. "He's scary."

"It'll be fine," said Jasmine, trying to sound confident. "He's just a grumpy old man. And we're not going to let a grumpy old man stop us from finding Pebble's family."

Chapter Thirteen
At Long Last

At five o'clock on Monday morning, Jasmine and Tom sneaked out of the house and walked back to the bridge.

The world was very quiet, the early morning peace interrupted only by birdsong. They stood there for half an hour, as the sky gradually grew lighter. Then Jasmine heard a little movement in the log pile. Tom turned towards her with a gleam of excitement in his eyes.

They fixed their gaze on the logs. There was a rustling in the undergrowth. Then a face

appeared. A broad, furry, brown face with bright black eyes and long white whiskers.

An otter!

At last, at long last, here was a real live otter, right here on the riverbank, right in front of them.

Tom beamed in rapture. Jasmine hardly dared to breathe. Could this possibly be Pebble's mother?

A little squeak came from the undergrowth.

Jasmine's heart thudded. She stared at the place where the otter had emerged.

There was another squeak. And then a furry brown face appeared from the log pile. A smaller face this time, followed by a smaller body.

A cub! A cub the same size as Pebble!

Jasmine turned to Tom, overflowing with joy. But Tom didn't look back at her. Somehow, without her even noticing, he had taken out his camera and was filming the otter and her cub.

She turned back to the otters. To her delight,

another cub appeared from the log pile. The
mother led them to a small patch of flattened
undergrowth a little way from the riverbank. The
cubs began to play fight, rolling over and over,
nipping each other with their tiny teeth. As they
wrestled, they made little squeaking sounds.

Jasmine and Tom stared in
wonder. *I can't believe we're
seeing this*, Jasmine thought.

Suddenly, the mother otter reared up on her hind legs, like a meercat, exposing her pale creamy throat and underside. She turned her head in all directions, her bright intelligent eyes watchful and alert. Jasmine froze. Had the otter somehow caught their scent? They were downwind of her, so she shouldn't be able to smell them.

After a few seconds, the otter lowered herself on to all fours again. Leaving her cubs rolling over and over, biting each other's tails, she lumbered towards the river and slid down the mud slide, pouring her sleek, lithe body almost soundlessly into the water. She dipped her head down, nosing below the surface. Then she arched her body and dived like a dolphin, disappearing into the depths. A few seconds later, she leapt up, shaking water from her whiskers, and raised her body half out of the water to look around.

Again Jasmine froze, terrified that the otter had caught their scent. But she lowered herself back

into the water and started nosing around just below the surface again. All they could see was part of her smooth back and her long thick tail.

She arched her body and dived. They followed the trail of bubbles until her head popped up. She was chomping noisily, revealing pointed fang-like teeth at the sides of her mouth. She had clearly caught something, but Jasmine couldn't tell what.

Tom filmed and Jasmine watched, fascinated, as the otter swam and dived and popped her head up again, chewing and crunching. All this time, the cubs never stopped their exuberant writhing and wrestling in their makeshift playpen.

And then the mother dived again. When she emerged, a small, wriggling, grey fish was clamped between her jaws. She swam to the bank, holding it in her mouth, and clambered up the mud slide. As she came towards her cubs, they stopped wrestling and started to make the same birdlike call that Pebble had been making

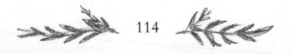

114

when Jasmine and Tom first found her.

The mother made the same call in reply. Then she dropped the fish at their feet. One cub immediately started eating, tearing at the fish and munching it. The other didn't seem very interested. It snuggled up next to its mother and sniffed her. Mother and cub started grooming each other and rolling around together, while the other cub continued to tear at the fish.

After a few minutes, the mother stood up and made for the mud slide, slipping into the water with barely a ripple. Again, she dipped and dived and nosed around in the water. She emerged with another fish, chewing and chomping. When she came up with a second fish, she swam to shore, climbed up on to the bank and released the fish beside the other cub. The first cub was still eating. The mother moved away from them and dried her fur, rolling on the ground and rubbing herself against the logs. She removed some bits of dirt from her fur with her claws.

Then she went back to her cubs, who were finishing their meal.

When they had finished eating, all three of them curled up together, grooming each other. One cub climbed on the mother's back and fell asleep. The other one started to suckle. When it finished suckling, it fell asleep too. Their resting place was surrounded by tall plants and flowers, making them invisible to anyone walking along the riverbank.

Eventually, the mother also closed her eyes. All three otters were fast asleep.

Jasmine looked at Tom, her eyes shining. "Wow," she mouthed. "That was unbelievable."

Tom lowered his camera. "Shall we go?" he whispered.

Neither of them spoke until they were well away from the river. Then Tom said, "That was the most incredible thing ever."

A wave of pure joy flooded over Jasmine. "I can't believe we found them! I can't believe

we've really found Pebble's family."

"We need to tell Neil," said Tom, "and then he can bring Pebble straight back."

"Let's phone Mum now," said Jasmine. "She can call him. She'll want to come and meet us to cross the road, too. You can send her the—"

Tom clutched her arm. "Oh, no," he said.

"What?"

She looked in the direction that Tom was looking.

"Oh, no."

An old man was striding across the field towards them, a thick stick in his hand and a furious look on his face.

"Hey, you!" he yelled. "How dare you trespass on my land?"

Chapter Fourteen
The Only People in the World

Angus Mizon was trembling with rage.

"You've got some nerve, strolling about like you own the place. Give me your names and addresses. I'm calling the police."

"Mr Mizon," said Jasmine, "we're Tom and Jasmine, and you told Mrs Thomas we could search for otters here. My dad's Mike Green, at Oak Tree Farm."

The old man stabbed his finger in Jasmine's direction. "I knew this would happen. I didn't want to give permission in the first place, but

she promised me it was only the once. I said to her, you let people come in once and they start taking advantage. Before you know it, you've got every Tom, Dick and Harry in the county thinking they can treat the place like a public park."

"It's not like that," said Tom. "Honestly it's not. We found a holt last night, and we just came back to watch for otters this morning. This is the last chance we've got to reunite the cub with her family."

"I never gave you permission to come here this morning. Give me your names and I'll call the police."

"We found otters," said Jasmine.

He snorted. "You think you found a holt, you mean. Well, you didn't. There've been no otters on this river for fifty years."

"Well, there are now," said Jasmine. "Show him, Tom."

Tom took out his camera. "We were standing

on the bridge down there," he said.

He pressed "Play" and handed the camera to Angus Mizon.

The old man stared as he saw Tom's footage of the otters emerging from their holt. He kept his eyes glued to the screen, watching the mother fishing in the river and feeding her cubs. He didn't move until the film had ended.

When he raised his eyes from the camera, his expression was a strange combination of boyish excitement mixed with a kind of sadness.

"I haven't seen otters on that river for half a century," he said. "Used to see them regularly when I was a boy. I'd come down here early in the morning and watch them for hours. Got to know where all their holts were, and when they had their cubs. Then the rivers got polluted, and what with that and the hunting, they all vanished. I never thought I'd see one again."

"And now they've come back," said Jasmine.

"All because you've kept your riverbank so lovely."

"This is the first otter family found in Sussex for forty years," said Tom. "And we're the only people in the world who know about it."

Angus Mizon grunted. "Well, it had better stay that way. I'm not having crowds of tourists trampling over my land, frightening them away."

"Of course not," said Jasmine. "We won't tell a soul. Except for Neil at the wildlife centre."

"Didn't you listen to a word I said? You're telling nobody."

"Mr Mizon," said Jasmine. "I promise that if you let us do this, we'll never set foot on your land again if you don't want us to. But the whole reason we've been searching for these otters is to reunite the lost cub with her family. You want her to be with her family, don't you?"

"I don't want a load of busybodies trampling over my farm," he said.

"It wouldn't be like that," said Jasmine. "Neil

said when they release an otter, they do it very quietly, and they don't reveal the location to anyone. The last thing they want is for people to come looking for otters and disturbing their habitats."

Angus Mizon was silent for a moment. Then he said, "Well, you'd better get this Neil person to give me a phone call. I'll see what he's got to say for himself. But I'm not having a load of idiots running about all over my land, and that's final."

"That is such an amazing achievement," said Mum, once she had seen them safely back across the main road, "that I might even forgive you for sneaking out of the house this morning. Although I can't ever forgive you for crossing that road on your own."

"It was really early," said Jasmine. "There weren't any cars around."

"Even so," said Mum. "It's not so much you I'm worried about, Jasmine, but I'm responsible for Tom at the moment."

"Oh, thank you very much," said Jasmine.

"That video footage is incredible," said Mum.
"I sent it to Neil and he wants you to phone
him as soon as possible."

They phoned as soon as they got back. Jasmine
dialled the number and handed the phone to
Tom.

"You should speak to him," she said. "You did
the filming."

"But it's your farm," said Tom.

"Go on. Put it on speakerphone, so I can hear."

But the voice that answered the phone wasn't
Neil's.

"Hemsley Wildlife Centre. Prunella Sharp
speaking."

"Oh," said Tom. "We thought this was Neil's
phone."

"It is. Neil is busy at the moment. Can I help
you?"

"This is Tom, from Oak Tree Farm," said Tom.

"You came to fetch Pebble, our otter cub. We've found her family and Neil asked us to call him."

"I think I already made it quite clear," said Prunella Sharp, "that we would not attempt the release of an otter cub at this stage."

Tom looked murderously at the phone. "Can we speak to Neil, please?"

"I'm afraid not. Neil is a very busy man."

"He asked us to call."

Prunella Sharp harrumphed like a horse. There was some indistinct murmuring in the background. Then Neil's voice said, "Hello, Tom. Sorry I was out of the room when you called."

He told them how thrilled he was with their discovery. "And your film footage is extraordinary," he said. "Amazing to see."

"Thank you," said Tom. His face was pink with pride.

"It's wonderful to see breeding otters back in this area," said Neil. "It's a great indicator of how much cleaner the rivers have become. Fantastic

124

news for wildlife."

"Will you bring Pebble back yourself?" Tom asked. "Or will it be Prunella Sharp?"

Jasmine pulled a face. *Please don't let it be Prunella Sharp*, she thought.

"Actually, Tom," said Neil, "I'm sorry to disappoint you, but I don't think we will be bringing Pebble back."

Tom's mouth fell open. Jasmine stared at the phone in disbelief. What was he talking about?

"I'm sorry," said Neil, "but we're not sure it would be a good idea to attempt a release."

"Why not?"

"It's just very unlikely that the mother will accept her back after three days."

"But you have to try," said Tom. "Why would you not try, when we've found her family?"

"Well, we don't know for certain that it is Pebble's family," said Neil. "I know it would be highly unlikely that there were two families with cubs the same age living on that stretch of river,

but we can't be sure. We don't want to stress Pebble by attempting a release, only for her to be rejected. After all, she might already have been rejected by her mother."

Tom said nothing. He looked utterly forlorn.

"I'm sorry, Tom," said Neil. "You should be very proud of yourself. You've made an incredible discovery and taken the most amazing footage."

Jasmine could bear this no longer.

"Give me the phone," she mouthed.

Tom handed it to her.

"This is Jasmine," she said to Neil.

"Oh, hello, Jasmine."

"If the mother does reject Pebble," Jasmine said, "she can go back to the centre, right? You said she's doing really well, so she'll be fine if she does. But it would be crazy not to

try. They always tell us at school to keep trying.
But you're just giving up without even trying
once. That's not a very good example to set for
children."

To her surprise, Neil laughed.

"Your mum told me you were strong-willed,"
he said. "I'm beginning to understand what she
meant."

"So will you try?"

There was a long pause.

"All right," he said, eventually. "I'll bring
Pebble to the location this evening. Dusk is the
best time for a release. Don't tell anyone except
your parents, OK? And I'll need to arrange
access. Can you give me the farmer's name and
number?"

Jasmine beamed at Tom in triumph.

"His name is Angus Mizon," she said.

"And he'll be happy for us to access his land?"

"Oh, yes," said Jasmine. "He'll be delighted."

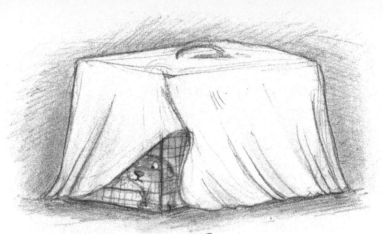

Chapter Fifteen
A Romp of Otters

Neil arrived at the farm just before eight o'clock that evening. When his van pulled up in the yard, Tom and Jasmine rushed out to see Pebble.

Neil opened the doors at the back of the van to reveal a cage covered in a blanket.

"It's best to keep it dark until we get to the location," he said. "She'll stay calmer that way."

"Can we have a quick look at her?" pleaded Jasmine. "Just to say hello?"

Neil lifted the edge of the blanket. Huddled in the corner of the cage, looking out at them with

big bright eyes, was the little otter.

"Hello, Pebble," whispered Jasmine. "It's so nice to see you again."

"Don't be frightened, Pebble," whispered Tom. "We think we've found your family."

Jasmine wished she could cuddle her, but she knew she couldn't. Pebble's mother would never take her back if she smelled of humans.

"Did you know a group of otters is called a romp?" said Neil.

"A romp of otters," said Tom. "That's exactly what they were."

To the astonishment of Jasmine's parents, Angus Mizon had insisted that Jasmine and Tom were present at the release. He came out of his house as they arrived. Neil introduced himself and Angus Mizon gave him a grim nod. Jasmine and Tom smiled at him and he nodded back, straight-faced.

"He doesn't want to ruin his image," Jasmine whispered. "He would have smiled if Neil wasn't here."

They set out across the fields, Neil carrying Pebble in her blanket-covered case.

"Shall we watch from the bridge again?" asked Jasmine.

"That's probably the best place," said Neil, "as long as the wind's in the right direction."

When they came to the field where they had seen the otters, Tom said, "See that bridge down there? That's where the holt is, on this side of the bridge."

"So if we stand on the bridge," said Neil, "we'll be downwind of the otters. We'll head across the top of this field until we're past the bridge, and then approach it from the other side. We can't risk our scent being carried on the wind."

They walked along the top of the field, next to the hedge. Once they were past the bridge, they began to walk down towards the river.

"You go up on the bridge," Neil murmured. "I'll release Pebble near the holt. I'm going to rub her with her bedding straw to disguise

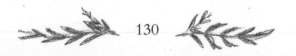

any human scent on her. Otters use smell to communicate, so we need to make sure Pebble only smells of herself. That way, her mum's much more likely to recognise and accept her."

Jasmine's heart beat fast as they stood on the bridge and watched Neil set down the cage. Please let this work, she pleaded silently. Please let this be Pebble's family, and please let them take her back.

Neil slowly removed the blanket, and Pebble looked around at her new surroundings. Tom was filming the scene. Neil pulled on a pair of thick gloves. He opened the top of the cage, grabbed handfuls of Pebble's bedding straw and rubbed her fur with it.

Still wearing the gloves, Neil picked Pebble up by the scruff of her neck and carried her towards the holt. He set her down a few metres from the entrance, away from the river. Then he joined Tom and Jasmine on the bridge.

They stood in silence, watching Pebble. She

reached her head up and looked around her. She took a few tentative steps across the grass. She looked hopelessly vulnerable, all alone on the riverbank.

Then she lifted her head up and gave a loud chirp. Jasmine held her breath. Would Pebble's whistle bring her mother out to find her?

Nothing happened. The riverbank was still.

Pebble whistled again. And this time, Jasmine was sure she heard a rustling in the undergrowth.

Pebble gave another whistle.

Leaves rustled. A twig cracked. And the broad brown furry face of the mother otter appeared from between two mossy logs.

Jasmine waited, her hands gripping the rail of the bridge. What would happen now?

The mother gave a loud whistle. Pebble whistled back. The mother reared up on her hind legs and looked around. Pebble gambolled towards her, chirping loudly. The mother got down on all fours and sniffed the cub. Pebble

jumped on to her back and the mother leaned round and sniffed her bottom. Then she sniffed Pebble's fur all over.

"If the mother licks her," whispered Neil, "we'll know she's accepted her."

Jasmine held her breath. Please let the mother recognise her, she thought. Please let Pebble smell right.

The mother rolled over on to her back. Pebble climbed on top of her. The mother licked her.

She recognised her! She knew this was her baby, and she was taking her back.

Neil grinned at the children and made a thumbs-up sign. Jasmine squeezed Tom's arm. "We did it!" she whispered.

"We did it," whispered Tom. "They're back together again."

From the holt emerged the little furry face of a cub just like Pebble. It gave a high-pitched whistle and scampered over to join its mother. Then the other cub's face appeared, and it ran towards its family.

The cubs jumped on their mother and started to play fight with Pebble, making funny little catlike growls and squeaks.

"They look like they're having so much fun," said Tom. "Pebble looks so happy to be back with her family."

"Yes," said Jasmine. "She really does."

Neil turned and smiled at them. "Congratulations, you two. This is pretty amazing."

It really was amazing, Jasmine thought. Everyone had said there was almost no chance it could happen. But it had happened. It was happening right now.

The mother rolled over and joined in the play fight. And then all four otters were rolling

around and chirping together on the riverbank, in the golden sunset glow. And the three people on the bridge stood and watched them, until the sun finally disappeared over the horizon and the last rays of light faded from the sky.

When Jasmine and Tom returned to the
farmhouse, Ella and Manu were sitting at the
kitchen table with Mum and Dad. Toffee and
Marmite were curled up in their basket by the
Aga stove. When Jasmine sat down, Marmite
uncurled herself, stretched luxuriously and
jumped on to Jasmine's lap.

"I've made hot chocolate," said Mum. "Would you like some?"

"And I made biscuits," said Manu, opening a cake tin.

"Terrifying," said Ella. "Who dares go first?"

"Don't be mean," said Mum. "They're not at all bad."

"Mum sent me some photos of the otter cub. She looked gorgeous," said Ella. "I got you something." She handed Jasmine a bag.

It was a beautiful otter cub toy, with silky brown fur, white whiskers and bright black eyes.

Jasmine got up and gave Ella a hug. "Thank you so much. I love her."

"It looks just like Pebble," said Tom.

"I'll call her Pebble, too," said Jasmine. "And whenever I look at her I'll be reminded of the real Pebble, living in the wild."

Manu handed Jasmine a biscuit and she took a very small bite. It was surprisingly nice. She took a bigger bite.

She thought of Pebble and her family on the riverbank, grooming each other and play fighting, so happy to be back together again.

Of course, Manu was deeply annoying most of the time. Probably Pebble's brother and sister were, too. But all in all, Jasmine thought, despite all the annoying bits, it was really quite nice to be part of a family.

Acknowledgements

I am very grateful to Charlotte Owens at the Sussex Wildlife Trust, Jason Palmer and the keepers at the New Forest Wildlife Park, and Jane Stevens at Mull Otter Group, for invaluable help and advice when I was researching and planning this story. Thank you so much for giving up your time to answer my questions.